FRE the Mouse™

Giving and Receiving

Book Four

Reese Haller

Written and Illustrated by
Reese Haller

PERSONAL POWER PRESS Inc.

Fred the Mouse™
Giving and Receiving
Book Four

© 2007 by Reese Haller and Personal Power Press, Inc.

Library of Congress Card Number
2007933173

ISBN - 978-0-9772321-5-4

Printed in the United States of America

Personal Power Press, Inc.
P.O. Box 547
Merrill, MI 48637

Cover Design
Foster & Foster, Inc.
www.fostercovers.com

Book Design
Connie Thompson, Graphics etcetera
connie2@lighthouse.net

Do You Have
Your Copy Of

Fred the Mouse™
Book One:
The Adventures Begin
by Reese Haller

Paperback book ($4.97) -
Available through Personal Power Press, Inc.
www.personalpowerpress.com - 877.360.1477 -
or from any bookstore nationwide.

The first book in the *Fred the Mouse™* Book Series
is written by 8-year-old author Reese Haller. Learn
how Fred uses his intuition and trusts his inner
knowing to stay out of trouble. This delightful book can be shared as a read-aloud with young children and as an independent reading book for second and third graders. *Fred the Mouse™: The Adventures Begin* is a Benjamin Franklin Award silver medal winner.

Fred the Mouse™
Book Two:
Making Friends
by Reese Haller

Paperback book ($4.97) -
Available through Personal Power Press, Inc.
www.personalpowerpress.com - 877.360.1477 -
or from any bookstore nationwide.

The second book in the *Fred the Mouse™* book
series by 9-year-old author Reese Haller. The
adventures continue as Fred befriends a snake,
barn swallow, crow, turtle, cat, and watchdog. A powerful story about the
importance of accepting diversity and uniqueness that even young children can
understand. *Fred the Mouse™: Making Friends* is a Mom's Choice gold medal
winner.

DEDICATION

I dedicate *Fred the Mouse*™ *Book Four: Giving and Receiving* to all those who have given of their time, talent, energy, and money to make our world a better place.

I thank my Aunt Jen and Uncle Marty for giving me the money for the first printing of *Fred the Mouse*™ *Book One: The Adventures Begin* two years ago. Their gift helped me share my love of writing, a passion that continues today.

I also wish to thank my mom and dad for teaching me the importance of giving and receiving.

For all of you who love the Christmas holiday as much as I do, thanks for giving.

Portraits by Mark Bradford

MY MISSION

I plan to touch the hearts and minds of millions of kids around the world and help them see that we don't have to wait until we are older to make a difference in the world.

We can write books, perform in the theater, present at conferences, create magical paintings, or even be a teacher.

I hope to inspire kids everywhere to be who they truly desire to be, now.

We are more than just the leaders of tomorrow, we are leaders today.

We can start now. It is time for the children of the world to release our inner genius and be who we were meant to be.

Visit Reese's Website: **www.reesehaller.com**

CONTENTS

Chapter 1

She's Ready

Fred woke with a start. His stomach lurched and tightened as it had thousands of times before. Fred had learned to respond to this feeling. It meant that something important was about to happen. He quickly stuck his nose in the air and began to smell its contents. He listened carefully and then he slowly poked his head out of his home under the tack room in the barn. Just as he did, a large black bird swooped down out of the sky. It was Fred's friend, Maggie.

"Hey, Fred," came a shout from Maggie's direction. But that was not Maggie's voice.

Fred recognized the voice and stepped out of his home. "Frank, is that you?"

"Yes, it's me, your crazy cousin."

Maggie giggled, "Frank's on my back, still hanging on for dear life. He screamed most of the way here." Maggie turned his head slightly to catch a glimpse of Frank still clinging to his feathers. "He said it was important and he needed to speak to you immediately."

Fred moved closer to help Frank as he slid off of Maggie's back. "Frank, I know you don't like to fly. This must be important. What's up?"

Grasping his chest and breathing heavily, Frank blurted out, "She wants out, she wants out!"

"What are you talking about?"

"The white mouse wants to come out of the cage."

"Whoa, slow down," interrupted Fred. "You mean to tell me the white mouse that we tried to set free from the glass cage this past summer wants out?"

"Yes," shouted Frank.

"Are you sure? We tried to set her free before and she wouldn't go. We even had a hole chewed in the top of the cage and she still wouldn't leave," replied Fred.

"We offered her the gift of freedom before and she chose to stay in the cage."

"Fred, we did give her freedom," interrupted Frank. "We gave her the choice to leave the cage or to stay. At that time she chose to stay, but now she wants out."

"Are you sure? I don't want to try to give something to the white mouse that she doesn't want," interjected Fred.

"I'm sure, but there's a problem. The people put a new cover on the cage and I can't chew through it. The white mouse and I have been trying for the last three nights. She definitely wants out and we need your help."

Maggie piped in, "I met two mice by the

dumpster at the school the other day. One of the mice goes to all the classes at the school. He's really smart. The other is a big strong mouse, one of the biggest I've ever come across. I bet I could get those guys to help."

"Good idea, Maggie," commented Frank. "We're going to need all the help we can get. Giving someone freedom is not easy. It's a lot of hard work."

That's all Maggie needed to know, and he launched himself into the air, calling out, "I'll be right back."

Fred and Frank scampered out of the winter cold and into Fred's cozy house. Frank turned to Fred, "I know you were sad the last time we tried to set the white mouse free and she wouldn't go."

A sad look overtook Fred's face as he remembered that day. "I really thought we were giving her what she wanted, but when she refused to do her part in getting out of the cage, I started to cry. I felt like she rejected our gift. We worked hard and put ourselves in danger and she still refused to leave."

"Yes, Fred, and in giving her that gift we got something back." Frank paused and took a deep breath, "We learned a valuable lesson about freedom that day. We truly gave the white mouse freedom. We gave her the freedom to choose, and she gave us a better understanding of what freedom really is."

Fred looked into his cousin's eyes, "I see what you mean, Frank. Whenever you give a gift you get something back. You're just not sure what you're going to get back until later."

For a few minutes all that could be heard was a gentle breeze blowing the fallen leaves outside of Fred's burrow under the tack room.

Frank interrupted the silence and spoke softly, "Fred, this time she's ready to be out of the cage. She wants the choice again."

Fred thought back to the conversation he'd had with his wise friend, Samuel, a few months ago. "I told Samuel, if she ever decides that she wants to leave, I'll give her the choice again, and that's what I'm going to do," Fred replied. "I hope she's serious about freedom this time."

"Oh, she is," replied Frank. "She is."

The two cousins sat quietly for several minutes thinking back to that day when the white mouse refused to leave the cage and the lesson they learned. Fred remembered Samuel teaching him about the concept of freedom and that it is all about having a choice. The white mouse was offered the gift of freedom before and she chose to stay. Samuel said at that moment the white mouse was truly free. She was free to choose to stay or choose to go, and in her freedom she chose to stay.

The silence was broken by Maggie's voice,

"Hey, guys, come out here. I've got someone I want you to meet."

Frank and Fred quickly popped out of the
mouse hole to see two mice standing next
to Maggie. The two were opposites. One
had a big round belly like a tennis ball
and stood almost as tall as the other. The
second mouse was skinny as a stick, with
a big smile on his face. He stepped for-

ward first.

"Good morning. My name is Steve. Most call me Skinny Steve because, . . . well, because I'm so skinny."

"Most call me Big Bob," (anyone who met Bob could tell why) interjected the other mouse, with what looked like a piece of cookie dangling from his whiskers. In a deep voice he continued, "And you are the famous Fred?"

Skinny Steve chimed in, "The scurry and scamper champion, the only mouse in history to ever outrun, outmaneuver, outsmart the mob of crows in the final exam."

"Hey, enough about that outsmarting us crows," interrupted Maggie. "Let's just say, he's the One and there won't be any others."

Fred stepped forward and quietly replied, "I'm Fred and this is my cousin Frank."

"Maggie told us about you, Frank. You used to be a field mouse and now you live in a house in the city," said Big Bob.

"In actuality, you live just around the corner from us," added Skinny Steve. "We live at the school in your neighborhood. It's a great place to learn."

"And eat," added Bob.

Maggie stepped closer, "I figured these two guys could help you. Skinny Steve, as I said earlier, is the smartest mouse I know. He spends most of his days in class with the kids at the school. He under-stands the humans' language and knows just about everything. Bob here is big, strong, and maybe even faster than you, Fred, when it comes to getting to the food first. The four of you ought to be able to set that white mouse free no matter what."

Skinny Steve stepped closer to Fred, "So, Maggie tells me that you tried to set this white mouse free before?"

"Yes," answered Fred. "But she refused to go. We offered her the gift of freedom, and in her freedom she chose to stay in her cage."

"That's what's interesting about gifts,"

said Steve wisely. "You never know what others are going to do with them and what you might get in return."

Bob interrupted, "I think of it this way, whenever I give somebody a cookie, I do it because I want to. I don't expect to get anything back."

"That's right, Bob," said Steve. "You give to give, not to get." He paused for a moment and then added, "So when we go to set this white mouse free again, let's not expect her to give us anything back. Let's all agree that we'll do it because we want to, and let the white mouse decide the outcome."

The four mice looked at each other and, without saying a word, nodded in unison.

Maggie turned, spread his wings, and shouted, "Climb aboard. Let's do this thing!"

Chapter 2

Return to the White Mouse

 The flight back to the city was difficult for Maggie. Four mice were hard to carry, especially when one of them was as heavy as two mice. Frank kept his eyes tightly shut through the entire flight, clutched his chest, and screamed from time to time. Big Bob became focused on the cookie crumbs in his whiskers and didn't pay attention to much else. Skinny Steve was going on and on about the cloud formations and what each meant and how much moisture they contained. Fred smiled as he always had since his first flight with Lou, the barn swallow.

The flight seemed to take longer than usual from Maggie's perspective, and he was happy to touch down in the front yard of Frank's city home. Still holding his chest, Frank jumped from Maggie's back first and yelled, "Follow me!"

He led the three mice to a crack in the side of the brick home. "Come on," he said, as he quickly slipped into the crack and out of sight.

Big Bob stepped forward and without hesitation worked his way into the crack. Steve gave a few nudges to Bob's behind with his shoulder, and soon Big Bob disappeared. Steve was fast on his tail, as if somehow Bob was pulling him along. Fred entered with a slight pause. "I hope she's ready," he whispered to himself.

Once all four mice were inside, Frank led them through the wall to a tiny hole just above their heads. "Fred, will you go first and check to see if the coast is clear?" asked Frank.

Fred stretched up and put his nose to the edge of the hole. He sniffed and waited a few seconds, being sure to check his feelings. Then he perked up his ears and listened. He checked his feelings once again. Sensing no danger, he slowly stuck his head through the hole and looked around carefully. He could see the cage sitting on a small table about three feet above him, but he couldn't see the white mouse yet.

Fred popped through the hole and with lightning speed climbed the side of the chair sitting next to the table. In a flash he found himself standing across from the white mouse. He remembered the first time he came nose to nose with the white creature and was shocked by her appearance. Now he had mixed emotions running through him. He was seeing her for the first time since she chose not to leave the cage several months ago. He stared at the cage, unable to move.

"Come on, Fred," whispered Frank as he tapped his cousin on the shoulder. "She wants out now. It's time to let go of the past. Just because she didn't accept your gift before doesn't mean it wasn't an act of generosity. Let's stay focused on getting her out."

Fred blinked, took a deep breath, and jumped to the table, joining Steve and Bob next to the cage.

Steve spoke first, "An albinistic mouse due to the lack of pigmentation. It is a rare disorder that can affect any creature. I've seen this in books at school."

The white mouse stepped closer so that she was directly across from Fred. "Fred, I'm ready now. Will you give me the choice again? I want to choose freedom."

"Yes," he replied. "That's why we're here."

"I've been gnawing on the cage lid for hours and it doesn't even make a dent," squeaked the white mouse.

"Let me take a look," interrupted Steve. "Give me a boost, Bob."

Big Bob grabbed Skinny Steve and effortlessly hoisted him up on his shoulders. Steve sniffed, gave the lid a few nibbles, and then jumped down. The four mice huddled together as Steve began giving directions. The white mouse waited.

After about five minutes the huddled dispersed. "Move that wheel thing over to this corner and jam it against your water bottle," yelled Steve to the white mouse. "Climb on top of it, and when I tell you, push up with all your might. Wait for the signal."

From the outside of the cage the four mice gathered in the same corner. Steve climbed on Bob's shoulders and Fred climbed on top of Frank's. Fred and Steve carefully positioned their paws on the edge of the heavy metal lid. "Are you ready in there?" shouted Steve.

"Yes."

"On three . . . ONE, TWO, THREE . . . PUSH!!!"

The corner of the lid popped up slightly. "Again!" yelled Steve. "And this time, when the lids pops up, you quickly slide through."

"ONE, TWO, THREE," yelled Steve, and they all gave out a big grunt.

Just as before, the lid popped up, but this time the white mouse was ready. She quickly dove for the crack between the top of the cage and the lid. The metal lid came slamming down once again, catching the white mouse on the lower back. "Push harder," yelled Fred. "Come on, white mouse, you can make it!"

She frantically clawed with her back legs as the edge of the lid scraped along her back, digging into her skin. She screamed as she fell, and the lid slammed shut behind her.

Fred quickly jumped from Frank's shoulders and caught the white mouse just before she hit the table. "You made it, you're out," he said softly, as he held her gently in his grasp.

"Hurry, out of sight in case the humans heard the noise," shouted Frank.

Big Bob grabbed the little white mouse and helped her to her feet. With Bob on one side and Fred on the other, the white mouse was ushered down the side of the chair and to the floor. Steve examined her back and tail. "No cuts, no bleeding, nothing broken. You might have a bruise or two come tomorrow."

"I feel wonderful," said the white mouse. "I'm out. I'm free! Thank you."

Fred smiled as a warm, tingling sensation in his heart began to arc through his body. The white mouse accepted his gift differently. Fred felt the acceptance of the gift and joy filled him.

Chapter 3

The Exploration Begins

 The white mouse tested her ability to move easily and comfortably by running around the outside of the group a few times. As she ran, Fred took note of their surroundings. "Hey, Frank, what's going on here? What are all these fancy boxes doing piled up all over the place? And what's that big tree doing in the house? Shouldn't it be outside?"

"I don't know," answered Frank. "They started bringing in this stuff a few weeks ago."

"They are probably celebrating the holiday," commented Steve in a matter-of-fact tone.

"Celebrating a what?" asked Frank and Fred in unison.

"Well, lots of people celebrate Christmas or Kwanza or Hanukah this time of the year," continued Steve. "Humans gather every year to give gifts to each other, eat big meals, and remember their spiritual background."

"Did you say big meals? I'm staying," drooled Bob. "Point me to the kitchen. This hard rescuing work has made me hungry. I could go for a snack right now." He turned and headed slowly in the direction Frank was pointing.

"Be careful, Bob. The humans could be coming around any time now," cautioned Frank.

"I'm fine. I'm around these humans all the time in the kitchen at the school. I know how to handle them. No big deal."

"I'll go with him," added Steve in a motherly tone. "He gets a one-track mind when it comes to food, and I'll keep watch." He scampered off to catch up to his round buddy.

The white mouse stood looking at Frank and Fred in disbelief. "You mean you just go wherever you want?"

"Sure," replied Frank. "And now you can, too. Where do you want to go?"

The white mouse stood quietly, not sure what to say. "I'll go with you," said Frank in a reassuring way.

"I don't know where to go. I've never been out of that cage, until now."

"Then let's go on an exploration. I'll show

you around the house where you have been living the past few years."

"I want to go check out that tree," said Fred. "I still don't get why that is in the house. You two go check out the rest of the house. I'm heading over there." He nodded his head in the direction of the big green tree in the corner.

Remembering the song his father taught him, Fred stopped to repeat it in his head.

First you put your nose up,
Sniff, sniff.
Then you put your ears out,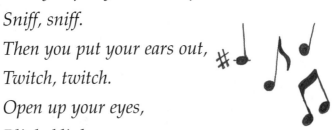
Twitch, twitch.
Open up your eyes,
Blink, blink.
Then we scurry and scamper.

Sensing that it was safe for him to go, Fred scurried out from under the chair and across the middle of the living room in the direction of the tree.

Frank nudged the white mouse, "Come on. Let's go this way!"

With the three groups of mice venturing in different directions, the exploration began.

Chapter 4

In The Kitchen

 By the time Steve caught up to him, Big Bob was standing in the middle of the kitchen looking at a tall cabinet with a protruding counter at the top. He kept sniffing the air.

"I smell cookies." *Sniff sniff.* "Chocolate chip." *Sniff sniff.* "Peanut butter crunch." *Sniff sniff.* "Sugar cookies with frosting on them." *Sniff sniff.* "Oh, I can't stand it any more. I'm going up there."

Immediately Bob started to climb. Steve stepped forward to give Bob a boost but it was already too late. Bob had hoisted himself to the first drawer and was using the edge of it to stand on as he stretched for the second drawer.

Having been on climbing adventures with Bob in the past where food was involved, Steve knew exactly what to do. Nothing stood between Bob and food, especially when the food was a cookie. The best approach was to get out of Bob's way and, of course, join him. Not to be left behind,

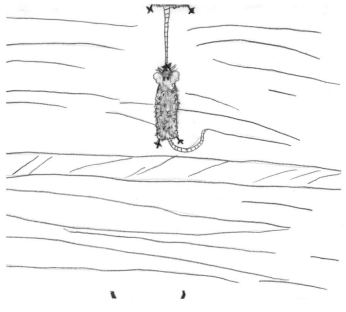

Steve jumped up as high as he could and grabbed the tip of Bob's tail. Bob didn't seem to notice. The extra weight didn't slow him down in the slightest. Steve held on tight with his front paws as his back legs struggled to find something on which to grip. Steve's footing didn't seem to matter much, Bob kept ascending regard-less, and so did Steve.

One drawer after another Bob climbed, gripping tightly with his tiny paws. The smell of the cookies increased as Bob, with Steve in tow, inched upward. As the smell increased, so did Bob's desire to bite into the sugary pleasure of a frosted cook-ie.

Steve could hear Bob breathing heavily as he was pulled past the third drawer. He called up to Bob, "Slow down. There is no need to rush. The cookies aren't going anywhere!" Worried, he let go of Bob's tail and rested on the third drawer, which was open slightly, making a small ledge on which to stand.

To Steve's surprise, Bob immediately stopped. "Hey, what's wrong, Steve? We're almost there. Don't give up now," shouted Bob from up above. "Come on, grab my tail, I'll get you there. We've climbed higher cabinets at the school before, and this time the prize is going to be worth it. I can tell by the smell."

Bob lowered his body a few inches and swung his tail in front of Steve, who grabbed a hold, and they were off once again. In a matter of minutes Bob reached the top, with Steve only a mouse tail behind. They both stood motionless at the top. In front of them was a tray of cookies the length across of five mice laying end to end. Bob's eyes were as big around as a chocolate chip, and drool dripped from each side of his mouth. Steve shook his head from side to side with his mouth hanging open.

The silence of the two mouse companions was broken by a thunderous roar from Bob's belly. The mountain of cookies towered over them like a stack of books on the school library floor. Bob wasted no time finding the sugar cookies, his favorite. He didn't stop at the first cookie he saw. He carefully examined each one, picking it up, sniffing around its edges, and sampling the frosting. He settled on a brightly frosted yellow star, thick in the middle and soft to the touch. Cookie in hand, Bob rolled on to his back, putting his feet in the air and resting the bottom of the cookie on his belly as he nibbled on the top.

Steve made his way to the opposite side of the cookie tray, where his favorite cookies, peanut butter, could be found. He broke off a large piece from one cookie and climbed to the center of the tray to join Bob.

"I'm in paradise," mumbled Bob with a mouth full of cookie.

Bob started to take another bite of his cookie when he stopped abruptly. "I have an idea. Let's share a little of this paradise with Frank, Fred, and the white mouse. I get a lot of enjoyment out of eating cookies, and I also enjoy sharing them with others. Gather up some pieces of your favorite cookies to give to them when we get back."

"Great idea! I can't wait to see the white mouse's face when she tastes a chocolate chip cookie for the first time," commented Steve with a smile on his face. "It will be fun for her and for us."

Cookie after cookie was tasted, and several pieces were set aside to give to the other mice. Bob searched for the best-tasting cookie to take back. It was an enjoyable search because it meant that he had to eat some of every cookie on the tray.

Steve found a small napkin on the countr and stacked the cookie pieces in the center. Bob and Steve slowly filled the napkin with tiny chocolate chips, green and red sprinkles, white-frosted cookie chunks, peanut butter cookie chunks, and a corner of the yellow star sugar cookie. When the napkin was filled with Bob's favorite selections, Steve folded the corners to the middle and tied a knot in them to form a handle for easy carrying.

As soon as the last knot was tied on the napkin, Bob immediately returned to his cookie eating. While taste testing several cookies, he discovered that taking a bite of a chocolate chip and then a bite of a peanut butter cookie and letting the two bites mix in his mouth made for a superb taste sensation. He was determined to recreate that experience and was on the

search for a big chocolate chip chunk to go along with the peanut butter piece he already had.

The cookie gift pile wrapped in a napkin seemed particularly inviting to Steve. Using the soft napkin as a head rest, he curled up next to the tiny pile, closed his eyes, and dozed off to sleep.

Steve wasn't asleep for long when he was startled awake by a loud crashing sound from the other room. "What was that?" he yelled as he jumped to his feet.

"I don't know. It sounded like glass breaking," whispered Bob, dropping his cookie. "Let's get out of here!"

Getting caught by the humans on the countertop without anything to hide under or behind was the last thing they wanted. Bob grabbed the napkin full of cookies and scurried for the counter's edge. Without hesitation he jumped. Having done this maneuver before, Bob pulled his legs close to his body as he fell to the floor. His tennis ball-like belly cushioned his fall, and he bounced several times before coming to a rest. As soon as he stopped bouncing, Bob stretched out his legs and ran to the nearest chair leg for cover.

Steve's descent was slightly different but almost as fast. He reached the counter's edge and grabbed the corner of the cabinet. With his right paws he held on to one side of the corner, while his left paws gripped the other side of the corner. Steve slid down the cabinet at the corner like a fireman sliding down a fire pole. His feet hit the ground running and he was right behind Bob.

The two mice scurried under the kitchen table and headed for the living room.

Chapter 5

In The Library

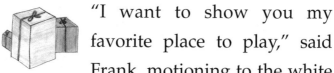

"I want to show you my favorite place to play," said Frank, motioning to the white mouse to follow him. "It reminds me of climbing rock piles when I used to live outside. Fred has a rock pile by his home that is just like this." They turned the corner and Frank motioned to the staircase that led to the second level of the house.

"Wow," exclaimed the white mouse in disbelief. "It's so high! We're going to climb that?"

"Yes, I'll show you how." Frank grabbed a

small gray loop of the carpet that covered the first step. "Look for loops sticking out like this and then use your back legs to push up while you pull. If you slip, you're still holding on to the loop and you can catch yourself." Frank pulled himself up and grabbed another loop with his other paw. He let go of the first loop and pushed with his back legs. He reached higher and grasped another loop. Frank repeated this process two more times before flopping onto the top of the first step. He looked down at the white mouse. "Now you do it."

Slowly she reached up and grabbed the first loop and pulled herself up while pushing with her back legs as Frank had described.

"Use your other paw to grab that loop right there," instructed Frank as he pointed to the loop to his right. "Keep going, one after another."

The white mouse followed Frank's instructions and reached the top of the first step in similar fashion. "That was fun," she said with a hint of excitement in her voice. "Let's do another one."

This time the white mouse went first while Frank gave instructions from below. At the next level up, the mice stopped and looked back at the climbing accomplishment. One step after another they climbed the stairs, taking turns going first. Higher and higher they went until they reached the last step to climb.

"Let's stop and catch our breath before this last one," panted Frank. They both sat down, and Frank turned to the white mouse. "You're a natural at this climbing. You would probably like it outside where there are many more objects to climb."

"I'm not sure what this outside world you talk about is like, but I sure do want to check it out," she replied. "I know you live here in the house, and Bob and Steve live inside, too."

"Yes, they live in a school."

"But Fred lives outside, right?"

"Yes."

"Well, do you think he would take me to experience the outside world?"

"I think so," replied Frank. "When we get back you can ask him." He paused for a moment and then added, "Once you've experienced being outside, you can decide where you want to live and make a new home for yourself there."

"I would like that," said the white mouse.

They sat quietly for a few more minutes before Frank jumped to his feet and said, "Come on, let's go up one more. I'll go first this time."

He reached up and grabbed a tiny loop and began to pull himself up. Frank stretched higher, with his opposite paw searching for something to grab. As he did, so he put his full weight on the loop below. The loop snapped under the pressure, which sent Frank tumbling down on top of the white mouse. She tried to catch him, but they both fell to the step below.

The momentum sent them tumbling down step after step like a ball of brown and white fur. They landed with a thud on the wood floor at the bottom of the stairs and slid to a halt on a patch of soft plush carpet across the hall. Their tails and paws were all tangled together as they lay quietly for a moment.

"Are you hurt?" asked Frank softly.

"No, I think I landed on you. Are you okay?"

"Yeah, I thought I landed on you," giggled Frank.

They untangled themselves and stood up slowly. They walked to the middle of the room in disbelief. Books covered all four walls from floor to ceiling.

"I've never been in this room before," said Frank. "The door is always closed and I haven't chewed a hole in the wall to get in here yet."

As they walked around the room looking at all the books, Frank thought he heard someone calling him. "Did you say something?" he asked the white mouse.

"No, I didn't say anything, but I heard something too," she replied.

They stood motionless and listened intently.

"There it is again. It's coming from over there."

Slowly and quietly they moved across the room until they could hear more clearly. It was a tiny voice.

"Hey, over here. Help me!"

They looked up and saw a tiny cage similar to the one the white mouse had been in. It was clear, with a wire mesh lid on the top.

"The voice came from in there," said the white mouse, pointing to the glass cage. Without a word, she raced up the first book shelf and jumped to the second row of books. Frank followed. The white mouse worked quickly as she searched for a row of books that tilted slightly, enabling her to climb the edge easier. It was as like she had climbed these books many times before, and yet this was her first time. Her determination inspired her, and in minutes she stood next to the glass cage.

Inside the cage was a thin creature with four small legs and a long tail. It was sticking to the side of the cage. It spoke first. "Can you help me get out of here? All you need to do is lift the lid slightly and I can squeeze out."

The white mouse glanced at Frank. "I want to set him free, just like you guys did for me. Do you think the two of us can do it?"

Frank examined the cage and its lid close-ly. "Yes, I think we can pry it up together. It looks like a smaller lid than what was on your cage." He looked up at the little creature and yelled, "Go to the corner, it will be easier for us there."

The little creature scooted across the glass as the white mouse climbed on Frank's shoulders. "Push up just like Steve showed us when we were at your cage," grunted Frank. "On the count of three, ONE . . .TWO . . .THREE."

The lid popped up only slightly, but the tiny creature was extremely quick and he zipped through the crack and jumped to a nearby book, clinging to the side of the cover.

"Hey, thanks, little mice. I've been trying to get out of that thing since they caught me a few weeks ago. Oh, excuse me for not introducing myself. My name is Juan. I'm an Anole and I'm from Southern Florida. I'm guessing by the lack of sun and the cooler temperatures I'm not in Florida anymore. I must be up north somewhere. Well, where's the warmest part of this place? Any ideas? You guys don't say much do you? I know my friends always say that I talk a lot, never give anyone else a chance to talk, maybe they're right, maybe not. Well, I'm off, I need to find some warmth. Point me in the right direction. I appreciate the help."

Frank cleared his throat. He had never seen a creature like this before and had never heard anything talk so fast. He spoke up slowly. "Downstairs is the furnace. It's hot down there. I can..."

"Great, come on, show the way," inter-rupted Juan. "Just point me in the right direction and I can do the rest. No need to hold my hand all the way. I got it covered. Let's go."

Frank looked at the white mouse, shrugged his shoulders, and scurried down the bookshelf, following the path they had come up. Juan zipped straight down the side of each book head first. Frank scampered out of the room and across the hall and into a small closet full of coats and jackets hanging from above. Juan and the white mouse followed. In the corner of the closet was a small hole. "Straight down that hole is the furnace room. It's always warm in there," said Frank.

Juan looked quickly down the hole and then back at Frank. "Thanks for setting me free and for the tip. Come and visit me. You're welcome in my home any-time." He turned and zipped down the hole. Frank and the white mouse could hear him talking as he went. His voice quickly softened as he descended. But they both knew he was still talking all the way down.

"Wow, that was cool," said the white mouse. "What a rush of joy I feel through my body. We just gave that little lizard freedom. Just like you guys did for me. Now I know what you must have felt when you set me free." She became quiet for a moment as she thought about her feelings. "I feel the same feelings now, after giving freedom, as I did earlier receiving freedom."

Frank smiled and put his front paw on the white mouse's shoulder. They stood silently together listening to the faint sounds of Juan's voice in the distance.

As they strained to hear his words, the silence was broken by an enormous crashing sound. Startled, Frank turned. "Hurry, follow me, something happened." He scurried out of the closet, past the steps, and rounded the corner towards the living room. The white mouse followed closely.

Chapter 6

In The Tree

 Fred weaved his way around several large boxes wrapped in colorful paper and topped with fancy bows and string. He reached the outer branches of the tree that were close to the ground where he stood. The tree smelled different, not like any tree he had smelled on the horse farm. He jumped up and grasped one of the branches to take a closer look. He noticed immediately that the branch did not bend as easily as the trees he was used to climbing. The green needles were not as sharp and had a smooth, shiny finish. He pulled himself onto the branch and sat gently bouncing up and down as he thought about this mysterious tree. Feeling the branch between his paws, he decided to find out what kind of taste the tree had. He bit down hard.

"Ouch," winced Fred. "That's not wood, that's metal!" He pulled back some of the green to find that the branch was actually silver wire. Fred crawled along the branch to the center of the tree to take a closer look at this strange object. At the center Fred tapped the trunk of the tree with his paw, and it too was metal. He reached up, grabbed a branch, and hoisted himself to the next level. Branch after branch was the same: metal, metal metal. *This tree is fake,* thought Fred. *It sure looks real, but there isn't anything real about it.*

Even more puzzled now than before, Fred climbed higher. The tree seemed to be filled with shiny objects, lights and bulbs that appeared to hang from a single thread at the tip of the branches. Interested in the dangling bulbs, Fred crawled to the outer edge of a limb where the largest bulb rested. He tapped it gently and it swayed back and forth before falling off the branch and sliding halfway down the tree. Curious, Fred followed.

He reached the bulb resting peacefully on two branches. He sniffed it. He carefully walked around the other side. He could see inside the object and almost through to the other side. He saw a tiny hole that seemed to lead into the object. Slowly, Fred poked his head inside. It was bigger inside than he thought. He squeezed his

body through the hole and easily found himself inside looking out.

Suddenly the bulb jerked. It slid through the branches and plummeted toward the ground. The smooth round shape of the bulb caused it to bounce slightly and start rolling across the floor. Inside, Fred tumbled head over tail. When the bulb finally came to a rest several feet across the room, Fred felt dizzy. His head was still spinning and he realized that this was not a safe place to stay. He immediately tried to squeeze back out of the hole, but for some reason he couldn't get his head through the opening. He was stuck inside.

He sat down in the middle of the bulb for a moment and cleared his mind so he could think the problem through. Peering through the bulb, Fred could see across the room to the table on which the white mouse's cage rested. He sat up and leaned to get a closer look. The bulb rolled forward. Fred took a step to collect his balance. The bulb rolled again. Fred realized that if he were to run inside the bulb he could move in any direction he wanted. He started running, and off he rolled. The bulb was difficult to control and it kept bumping into packages as Fred ran. On one occasion, he even ran into the wall with a thud, causing him to stumble.

As he pulled himself to his feet, he saw a small crack in the bulb. This gave Fred an idea.

Looking around the room for a clear running, rolling path, Fred moved the ball slowly away from the wall. He was able to get several feet away with a straight shot at the wall. Fred surged forward and in a few steps was running at top speed straight at the wall. The bulb shattered as it struck the wall, and Fred was free.

The loud crashing noise startled him. He was free from the glass ball, but the humans might have heard the noise. Fred immediately thought of Bob and Steve in the kitchen and Frank with the white mouse in the other room. He brushed the shattered glass pieces from his fur and looked across the room at the tree. *I might be able to see if they're okay from the top of the tree*, thought Fred. He ran as fast as he could across the living room, dodging packages as he went. Reaching the base of the fake tree, Fred jumped and started frantically climbing. Grasping limb after limb, he reached the top in seconds.

The top of this mysterious tree was flimsy and began to bend from the weight of

Fred's body. He held on tight as he struggled to regain his balance. He could easily see all the way into the kitchen, and he caught a glimpse of Bob diving off the countertop and bouncing across the floor. He saw Steve and Bob disappear under the kitchen table.

At the same time, Fred spotted the white mouse. Her white body was much easier to see as she ran across the open floor. Ahead of her was Frank. He stopped at the corner and looked cautiously into the living room. That's when Fred spotted the humans.

Chapter 7

Giving and Receiving

Two human children came running around the corner and headed straight into the living room. They were running so fast that they didn't even notice Frank and the white mouse lying as flat as possible at the base of the wall. Skinny Steve and Big Bob hid behind a chair leg under the kitchen table. Steve saw Frank along the wall, and as soon as the children passed he waved to them to join him under the table. Frank nodded to the white mouse and the two of them wasted no time cutting across the kitchen floor.

As soon as Frank reached Steve and Bob, he said, "We've got to keep moving and get out of this area. The adults will be coming, and then it will be hard to move anywhere. Hurry, let's go now and get under the couch over there." The four mice took off in a flash.

Fred saw the children as they ran around the corner of the kitchen, and he immediately let go of the tree top. He fell from branch to branch, tumbling off the edge of each and on to the next level below. The branches were surprisingly soft on the outer edges and they cushioned his fall as he plummeted. Fred rolled off the last branch to the carpeted floor just as the children entered the room. He quickly ducked behind the nearest box and looked for the closest cover. He saw Frank and Steve dart for the opposite end of the couch, so he headed for the couch as well.

The five mice met at a mid point under the couch. They all fell to the ground, gasping to catch their breath. The human children were so fixed on the presents that the activity of the mice went unnoticed. Breathing heavily, the mice remained huddled under the couch out of sight. As Frank predicted, the young children were soon joined by a few older children and several adults. The room quickly filled with the sounds of laughter, giggling, and the rustling of the humans' feet.

The mice settled in and began talking about their exploration. "Where were you guys?" asked Steve.

"We were in this room where all the walls were lined with books," answered Frank.

"Oh, they have one of those at the school. They call it the library."

The white mouse quickly joined the conversation. "We found another cage like the one I was in. In it was a weird-looking green creature. His name is Juan and he said that he was an ano . . . ano . . ."

"An anole? A little four-legged lizard from Florida probably," interrupted Steve.

"Yes," said Frank. "We set him free and then showed him the furnace room. He sure could talk fast."

While the others shared their adventures,

Fred watched the humans in amazement. They were giving the wrapped boxes to each other and watching each other open the boxes and share what was inside. Fred noticed that when one would open a box, a smile would appear on two faces. One smile was on the face of the person who opened the box and one on that of the person who gave the box. The people seemed just as happy to give a gift to someone else as they were to receive a gift from someone. Fred didn't completely understand why both people were happy.

Just then Bob dropped the napkin down in the middle of the group. "I've got something for you guys." He untied the napkin and the contents rolled out. "Cookies," shouted Bob. He reached in and grabbed the yellow star chunk. "This one is my favorite, Fred. Give it a try." He handed Fred the yellow-frosted cookie. As Fred reached for the cookie, he looked at Bob, who was smiling from ear to ear. Fred nibbled the cookie and watched Bob hand pieces of cookie to Frank and the white mouse. Bob was grinning the entire time.

Fred thought harder. He looked at the

humans smiling as they gave gifts and he looked at Bob as he gave his gifts. Back and forth he watched the face of Bob and the faces of the humans until he finally motioned to Steve.

Steve walked over to where Fred was sitting. "What's up, Fred?"

"Steve, why is Bob so happy when he gives me a piece of a cookie? Why are these humans as happy to give a gift as they are to receive a gift? I don't understand."

Steve sat back and scratched his chin. "Interesting observation you've made, Fred. You have noticed an important part about giving and receiving. I remember a discussion a teacher had with her class about this back at my school. The class was talking about the old saying, "It's better to give than to receive." What you have noticed in Bob and in the humans is that the saying is not true. Giving is not better than receiving. Giving and receiving are the same."

"How so?" interrupted Fred.

Not bothered by Fred's interruption, Steve continued, "You have to receive someone's willingness to give and give your willingness to receive. In other words, to accept a gift from someone else is also giving that person a gift back, the gift of acceptance. Giving and receiving are in balance. When a gift is received, the person who gave the gift gets something back, a feeling of acceptance." Steve paused and then added, "Think back to how you felt the moment the white mouse was free. You felt pretty good inside, didn't you?"

"Yes, I did," replied Fred.

Steve remained silent as he noticed Fred still thinking.

"Let me see if I've got this straight," continued Fred. "When Bob gave me his favorite cookie, he became happy when I took it because I accepted his gift. So I actually gave him a gift, too, just by receiving it."

"Yes, that's the balance of giving and receiving," replied Steve.

"Wow," said Fred in amazement. "Last summer, when I attempted to set the white mouse free, I learned an important lesson about freedom. This time I learned a valuable lesson about giving and receiving. Thanks, Steve."

Fred went back to watching the humans and enjoying another round of cookies offered by Bob. The day passed quickly and the humans moved to other areas of the house, some to the kitchen to begin making a meal and others to bedrooms to play with their toys. No one noticed the empty cage in the corner of the living room.

The five mice remained under the couch and talked about the rescuing of the white mouse and of the lizard in the library. It was mentioned that the lizard had a name, Juan, and that perhaps it was time for the white mouse to have one, too.

"I'm not sure what name I want," she replied. "But when I feel it, I'll know it. I'll wait for the feeling to come and I'll let you know."

The group agreed.

Bob quickly changed the subject when the smell of the dinner began to fill the air. "I think I'm staying for dinner. Anyone care to join me?"

"Yes," replied Steve and Frank in unison.

"I guess you two are heading outside?" Frank asked Fred and the white mouse.

"Well, if it's all right with you, Fred, I'd like to experience the outside world. Can I come with you to the horse farm?" the white mouse asked softly.

"Yes, I would like that very much," replied Fred. "Follow me, I'll show you the way out."

Frank, Steve, and Bob hugged the white mouse and wished her their best as she followed Fred down the little hole in the living room. The three stood silently staring at the hole. "I hope to see those guys at the school," commented Steve as a way to break the silence.

"Oh, you will," said Frank. "You will."

The white mouse followed Fred down the

inside of the wall and watched him as he slipped through a small crack and disappeared into the light on the other side. She took a deep breath, closed her eyes, and squeezed through the opening in the brick wall. She could feel a cool breeze across her whiskers as she fell to the soft earth.

She felt Fred gently lift her to her feet. "It's okay. You can open your eyes," he gently instructed.

She gasped at the wonder of what she saw. An enormous landscape of green grass and patches of white snow lay before her. A vibrant blue sky was graced with puffs of white clouds. She smiled and looked peacefully at Fred. "This is freedom! I am free!"

"Yes, you are truly free," replied Fred softly.

"To remember this day and what you gave me, I wish to no longer be called white mouse. My name is . . . .

Chapter 8

The Name

 ... Freedom!"

**Mice
And others
From**

FRED
The Mouse™
Giving and
Receiving

FRED: The mouse scurry and scamper champion from *Book One: The Adventures Begin*. Not only is he the fastest mouse ever seen at the Mouse Scurry and Scamper School, he also has a unique ability of trusting his intuition.

FRANK: A field mouse who is Fred's cousin. He moved out of the field in *Book*

Three: Rescuing Freedom and became a house mouse.

MAGGIE: The largest member and leader of the "Mob of Crows." He is a close friend of Fred's and enjoys flying with his mouse companion on his back.

BIG BOB: A gray mouse that lives in a neighborhood elementary school. He is tall, strong, and has a big belly like a tennis ball.

SKINNY STEVE: A gray mouse that lives in a neighborhood elementary school. He is extremely smart from attending classes with the kids and is rather thin.

THE WHITE MOUSE: An albino mouse that Frank and Fred attempted to set free in *Book Three: Rescuing Freedom.*

JUAN: A fast-talking, swift-moving anole.

ABOUT THE AUTHOR

Reese Haller
Author/Lecturer

Reese is ten years old and a sixth grader at Handy Middle School in Bay City, Michigan. He is considered one of the youngest published fiction authors in

America. Reese began writing short stories in kindergarten, where he was encouraged to take risks with his writing. He discovered his joy and passion in the third grade, where he blossomed as a writer.

While at the age of eight, before entering fourth grade, Reese wrote his first book,

Portraits by Mark Bradford

Fred The Mouse™ Book One: The Adventures Begin. It is a Benjamin Franklin Award silver medal winner. He wrote **Fred the Mouse™ Book Two: Making Friends** during his Christmas break in December 2005. Book Two is a Mom's Choice Award Gold Medal Winner. Reese wrote **Fred the Mouse™ Book Three: Rescuing Freedom,** which was nominated for a Newbery Award, during the summer before entering fifth grade. **Fred the Mouse™ Book Four: Giving and Receiving** was written during the summer before Reese entered the sixth grade. For more information visit Reese at www.reesehaller.com.

Reese has been a regular presenter at elementary schools across the country, since 2005, where he lectures on how to inspire children to write in a captivating 45-minute presentation entitled, **Catching the Writing Bug: From One Kid to Another.** He has presented live to over 15,000 people through teacher in-services, keynote addresses, and numerous elementary classrooms talks discussing writing and publishing. In September 2007, Reese appeared live on The Martha Stewart Show, reaching thousands with his message about writing and reading.

On March 19, 2006, Reese was appointed the

Ambassador of Literacy for the Youth of Michigan by Michigan's Governor, Jennifer Granholm.

Reese has also been appointed to the National Advisory Council for the Statue of Responsibility, a United States national monument, to be unveiled in July of 2010. He is a featured author, along with Oprah, Stephen Covey, Barack Obama, Pope John Paul, George S. McGovern, and fifty-five other authors, in a book to support the national monument entitled *Responsibility 911*. For more information on the Statue of Responsibility, visit www.sorfoundation.org.

 # Reese's Charity

I am donating a portion of the proceeds from my *Fred the Mouse*™ Book Series to **Healing Acres Equine Retirement Ranch, Inc.,** for the purpose of establishing a reading library at the ranch.

My goal is to create a library and maintain a reading program at **Healing Acres** where children have the opportunity to read with a horse or about a horse while they are visiting the ranch. I envision a place where children can read about how to care for a horse and then have a chance to touch, brush, feed, and even ride a real horse. I chose a wall in the barn that I want to turn into bookshelves so people have a variety of reading choices about horses.

As a way to remember their experience, I will give to every visitor, young and old, a book about horses to take home.

I want every child to have the opportunity to experience the same joy I experience every day: the joy of reading and the joy of being with horses.

If you wish to make a donation beyond the purchase of this book, please visit: www.healingacres.com.

Thank you for helping me create my dream.

HOW TO INVITE REESE TO YOUR SCHOOL

Would you like Reese to come to your school for a Literacy Day?

It's easy. Just e-mail Reese at reese@reesehaller.com and ask about available dates for a Literacy Day.

You can also call Personal Power Press toll-free at **877-360-1477** and ask about scheduling Reese for a Literacy Day.

When you schedule a Literacy Day, your school receives:

• Reese for the entire day presenting the 8 steps of writing that he developed for writing his books. A presentation entitled **Catching the Writing Bug: From One Kid to Another.** A DVD of Reese's presentation can be purchased on his website at www.reesehaller.com.

• Signed copies of *Fred the Mouse*™ books

- A parent evening workshop where Reese and his dad give parents practical strategies and fun exercises that will inspire a love of writing in children.

INVITE REESE TODAY!!

www.reesehaller.com

NOT ABLE TO BRING REESE TO YOUR SCHOOL?

No problem.

Reese's presentation is now available on DVD!

In this power packed instructional DVD Reese presents his eight steps of writing. At the conclusion of each step Reese offers tips and writing exercises for teachers to use in the classroom.

ONLY $24.95

Purchase a copy for your school or home today at www.reesehaller.com.